Princess! Fairy! Ballerina!

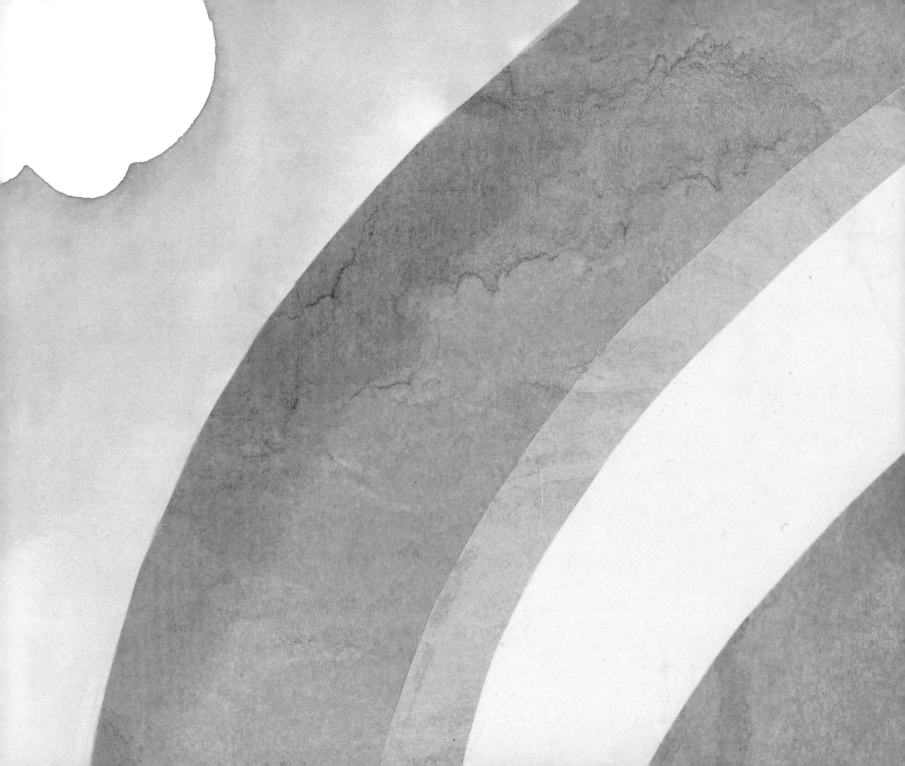

Princess! Fairy!

Ballerina!

by BETHANIE DEENEY MURGUIA

SCHOLASTIC INC.

Greetings!

Hugs!

Hello!

What should we play?
I'm ready for magic.

Let's put on
a grand show!

I know what
we'll do!

We shall play princess!
Because princesses are *royal*,

and that means they get to
survey their royal domains,

and make the royal rules,

Dragons shall
not breathe
fire—
only clouds.

All flowers
shall be blue.

The royal
moat shall
have three
waterslides.

All parades
shall include
unicorns.

The royal
ice cream
parlor sh

and, of course, ride the royal unicorns.

You *always* want to play princess.

Please, call me *Your Majesty*.

Shh, I have two words for you —

Fairy. Dust.

Because fairy dust
means magic spells,
and talking frogs,

May I have this dance?

and flying over rainbows.

Frogs?
Frogs are
not royal.

But real
princesses
kiss frogs.

Ahem.
We should
play *ballerina*.

Ballerinas can be beautiful snowflakes or fierce mice.

Sometimes they're graceful swans,

soaring high above the stage as the audience cheers!

It could be a
flying contest.

Or a throne-sitting
contest.

How about a
balancing contest?

Parade leading.

Toe pointing.

Magic making.

Twirling!

Crown weaving!

Tea-and-crumpeting!!!

CRUMPETING?
That's not even a word.

It is in MY kingdom.

LISTEN!
We should play —

Princess! Fair!

Ribbit.

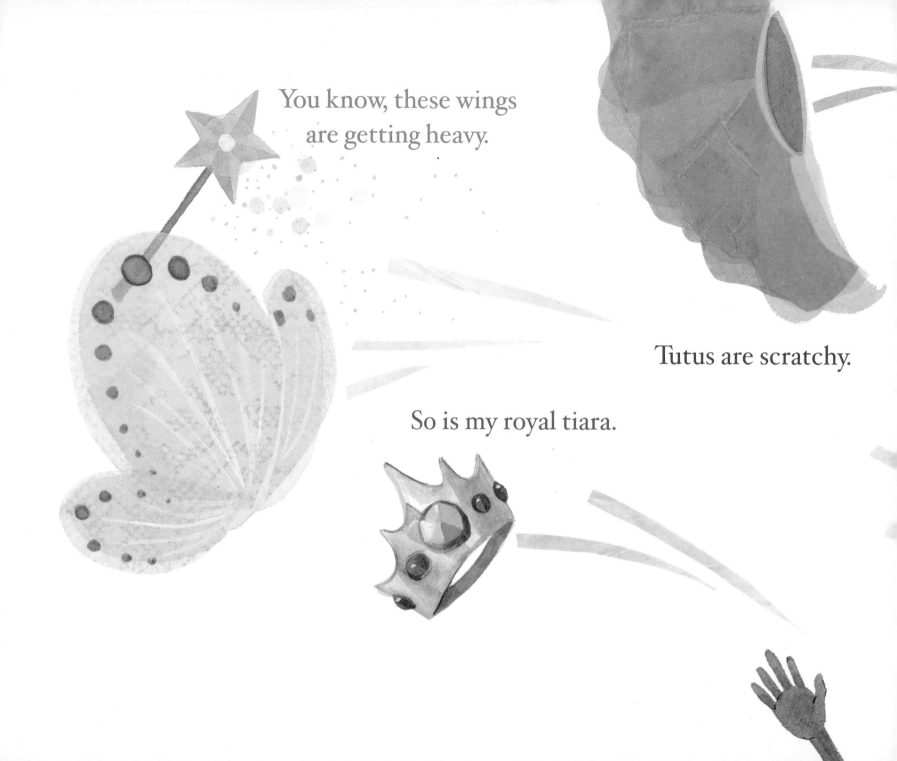

You know, these wings
are getting heavy.

Tutus are scratchy.

So is my royal tiara.

Who needs
dust to fly?

Our best performance yet!

I declare this day a royal success!

For all of the princesses, fairies, and ballerinas
who are writing their own rules, finding their own magic,
and dancing their own dances.
—B.D.M.

Bethanie Deeney Murguia

has illustrated ten wonderful picture books, including *Zoe Gets Ready*, *Zoe's Room (No Sisters Allowed)*, and *Zoe's Jungle*. As a parent, Bethanie has become well versed in all things princess-fairy-ballerina, inspiring her to write a story about the joys and limitations of these personas. She lives in Sausalito, California, with her family and her very own wings and wand.